Wildlife Preserves

Other Books in The Far Side series

The Far Side
Beyond The Far Side
In Search of The Far Side
Bride of The Far Side
Valley of The Far Side
It Came from The Far Side
Hound of The Far Side
The Far Side Observer
Night of the Crash-Test Dummies
Wiener Dog Art
Unnatural Selections
Cows of Our Planet
The Chickens are Restless

Anthologies

The Far Side Gallery
The Far Side Gallery 2
The Far Side Gallery 3
The Far Side Gallery 4

The PreHistory of The Far Side:
A 10th Anniversary Exhibit

Wildlife Preserves

A Far Side Collection

by Gary Larson

WARNER BOOKS

A *Warner* Book

ISBN 0 7515 0422 X

Printed and bound in Great Britain by
BPCC Hazell Books Ltd
Member of BPCC Ltd

Warner Books
A Division of
Little, Brown and Company (UK) Limited
Brettenham House
Lancaster Place
London WC2E 7EN

Wildlife Preserves

Life in the primordial soup

"Well, we've done everything we can; now we can only wait and see if she pulls through. ... If she doesn't, however, I got dibs on these ribs right here."

Karl Malden in his basement

Cowmen Miranda

Moses as a kid

"So then I says to Borg, 'You know, as long as we're under siege, one of us oughta moon these Saxon dogs.'"

Suddenly, Dr. Morrissey's own creation, a hideous creature nine feet tall and bearing the heads of the Brady Bunch, turns against him.

Early settlers of Beverly Hills

Slowly he would cruise the neighborhood, waiting for that
occasional careless child who confused him
with another vendor.

Construction birds at lunch

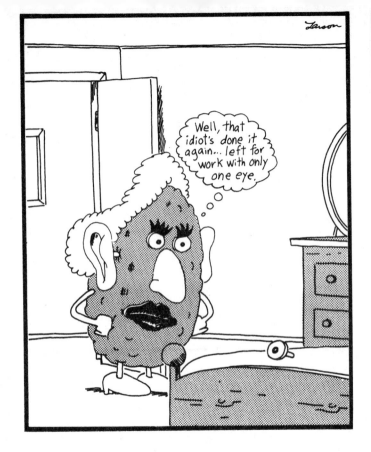

More Facts of Nature: As part of nature's way to help spread the species throughout their ecological niche, bison often utilize a behavior naturalists have described as "ballooning."

Early kazoo bands

Anatidaephobia: The fear that somewhere, somehow, a duck is watching you.

Tethercat

"Just look at this room — body segments everywhere!"

The matador's nightmare

Primitive fraternities

"I don't know if this is such a wise thing to do, George."

"You know, Vern...the thought of what this place is gonna look like in about a week just gives me the creeps."

"Yo! Everyone down there! This is the jackal! I'm tired of slinking around in the shadows! ... I'm coming down to the kill! Is that gonna be cool with everyone! ... I don't want trouble!"

"Careful, Lyle! ... There's some cattle dancing!"

"Did you detect something a little ominous in the way they said, 'See you later'?"

"I tell you I've *had* it! ...I'm not climbing into that getup one more time until you tell me why I'm always the *back* end!"

"Drive, Ted! We've stumbled into some cowtown."

"*Sure* it's true! ... Cross my heart and hope to die, stick a sharp chunk of obsidian in my eye."

The Potatoheads in Brazil

Bombardier beetles at home

"We understand your concern, ma'am — but this just isn't enough for us to go on. Now, you find the *other* half of your husband, and then we've got a case."

Mobile hobbyists

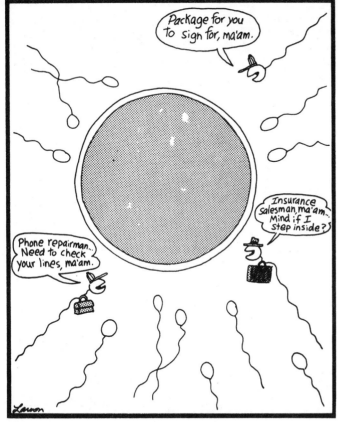

How the human egg is often deceived.

Frog pioneers

"Aha! The murderer's footprints!
'Course, we all leave tracks like this."

"Hey! Ernie Wagner! I haven't seen you in, what's it been — 20
years? And hey — you've still got that thing growin' outta your
head that looks like a Buick!"

"Good heavens, Bernie! We've got company! ...
And you're never going to catch that stupid squirrel anyway!"

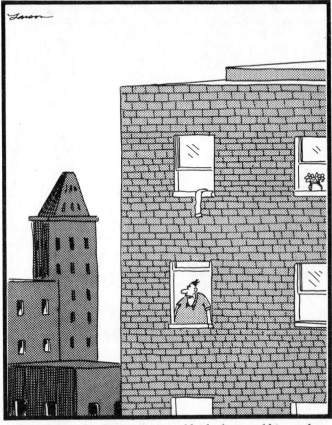

On a clear day, Eugene rose and looked around him and,
regrettably, saw who he was.

Headhunter hutwarming

"Oh, good heavens, no, Gladys—not for me.
...I ate my young just an hour ago."

Nonunion wagon masters

"Oooooooweeeeee! This thing's been here a looooooooong time.
Well, thank God for ketchup."

"OK, when I say 'draw,' we draw. ... Ready? ... One, two, three — STRAW! ... OK, just checkin' your ears. ... One, two, three — CLAW! ... OK, DRAWbridge! ..."

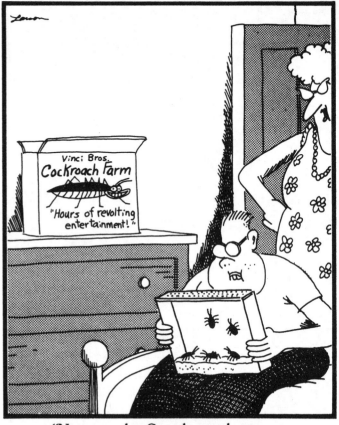

"Now remember, Cory, show us that you can take good care of these little fellows and maybe *next* year we'll get you that puppy."

Splattered with juice and hooting excitedly, Neanderthals are depicted here as they proceed to carve up their favorite kill, the woolly watermelon.

Hell's Cafeteria

Scene from *Return of the Nose of Dr. Verlucci*

Why people named Buddy hate to drive

"What? You're just going to throw the tail away? ... Why, in *my* day, we used every goldang *part* of a mammoth!"

The Fullertons demonstrate Sidney's trick knee.

Sucker fish at home

As the cactus stood watch over the sun-drenched land, a red-tailed hawk hung motionless in the desert sky. Little stirred, except an occasional lizard scurrying for shade or a tumblenerd drifting by.

"Why, thank you. ... Thank you very much!"

"I can't believe it! This is impossible! Nothing here but — wait! Wait! I see something! ... Yes! There they are — granola bars!"

"Hold it right there, young lady! Before you go out, you take off some of that makeup and wash off that gallon of pheromones!"

Street physicians

Embedded in Styrofoam "shoes," Carl is sent to
"sleep with the humans."

"I built the forms around him just yesterday afternoon when he fell asleep, and by early evening I was able to mix and pour."

"Pretty cool, Dewey. ... Hey! Shake the jar and see if they'll fight!"

"Mr. Cummings? This is Frank Dunham in Production. ...
We've got some problems. Machine No. 5 has jammed, several
of the larger spools have gone off track, the generator's blown,
and, well, everything seems to be you-know-what."

Aug. 11, 1957: Tito Puente loses the beat

Nov. 3, 1963: Ella Fitzgerald hits a flat note

Sept. 9, 1948: Dizzy Gillespie can't find Bb

July 14 1974: Oscar Peterson forgets the chords to "Heart and Soul."

Infamous moments in jazz

"Well, thank God we all made it out in time.
... 'Course, now we're equally screwed."

"Hey, Bob...did I scare you or what?"

"Bobby, jiggle Grandpa's rat so it looks alive, please."

"So...they tell me you're pretty handy with a gun."

Mountain families

Hummingbirds on vacation

Fruitcakes of the World

Butterfly yearbooks

"Oh, for heaven's sake, Miss Carlisle! ...
They're only cartoon animals!"

Primitive think tanks

Fly travelogues

Her answer off by miles, Sheila's "cow sense" was always a target of ridicule.

The famous "Mr. Ed vs. Francis the Talking Mule" debates

Scene from *Bring 'Em Back Preserved*

Goldfish laundry days

"Yeah, yeah, buddy, I've heard it all before: You've just metamorphosed and you've got 24 hours to find a mate and breed before you die. ... Well, get lost!"

"All right! Hand me the tongs, Frank. ... We got us a big den of rattlers here."

Aladdin's lamp, end table, and sofa

Monster jobs

"You and Fred have such a lovely web, Edna —
and I *love* what you've done with those fly wings."

Professor Feldman, traveling back in time, gradually succumbs
to the early stages of nonculture shock.

"The wench, you idiot! Bring me the *wench*!"

"Well, this may not be wise on a first date, but I just gotta try your garlic wharf rats."

The world was going down the tubes. They needed a scapegoat. They found Wayne.

June 2, 1952: Naturalists discover the Secret Chipmunk Burial Grounds.

"Well, the Sullivans are out on their tire again."

"Hold it! There's a car across the street — you sure
you weren't followed, Mary?"

"Well! No wonder! ... Look who's been
loose the whole evening!"

"And this report just in. ... Apparently, the grass
is greener on the other side."

Cockroach nightmares

The toaster divers of Pago Pago

The untold ending of D.B. Cooper

Robby works his ant farm.

"You want me to stop the car, Larry, or do you want to take
your brother off the rack this instant?"

An instant later, both Professor Waxman and his time machine are obliterated, leaving the cold-blooded/warm-blooded dinosaur debate still unresolved.

Michelangelo's father

Saloon scenes on other planets

Full moon and empty head

"Now relax. ... Just like last week, I'm going to hold the cape up for the count of 10. ... When you start getting angry, I'll put it down."

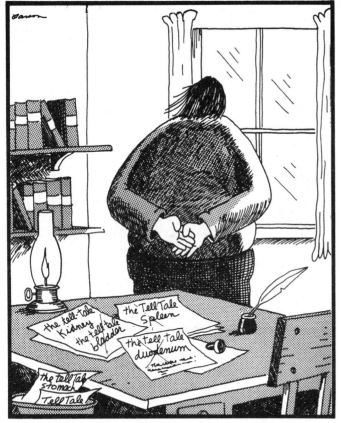

Edgar Allan Poe in a moment of writer's block

The elephant man meets a buffalo gal.

The big-lipped dogs of the equatorial rain forest

Young Victor Frankenstein stays after school.

"Let go, Morty! Let go, Morty! You're pulling me in!
... Let go, Morty! You're pulling me in!"

"Well, it's cold again."

"What the? ... This is lemonade! Where's my culture of amoebic dysentery?"

"Man, this is havin' no effect. ... But if the boss wants this varmint dragged through the desert, I ain't gonna argue."

"Well, well — another blond hair. ... Conducting a little more 'research' with that Jane Goodall tramp?"

"Not bad, but you guys wanna see a *really* small horse?"

"No, no, no! What are you doing? ... Fifth leg! Fifth leg!"

"That does it, Sid. ... You yell 'tarantula' one more time and you're gonna be wearin' this thing."

And by coincidence, Carl had just reached the "m's."

Early archaeologists

Crossing paths on their respective journeys of destiny, Johnny Appleseed and Irving Ragweed nod "hello."

Roger crams for his microbiology midterm.

"Tell it again, Gramps! The one about being caught in the shark frenzy off the Great Barrier Reef!"

Accountant street gangs

Just when you thought it was safe to go back into the topsoil.

The fake McCoys

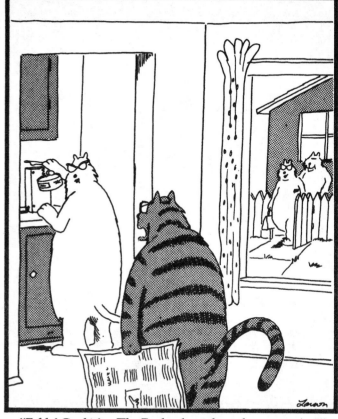

"Zelda! Cool it! ... The Rothenbergs hear the can opener!"

Inexplicably, Bob's porcupine goes flat.

"Carl, maybe you should just leave your flashlight off. We're
trying to scare these kids, not crack 'em up."

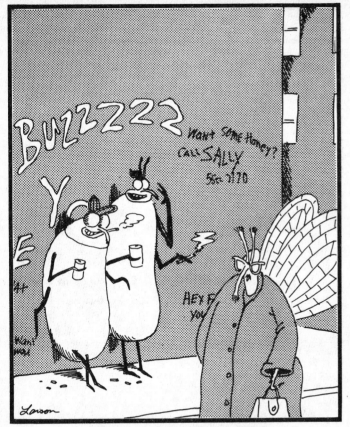

Killer bees are generally described
as starting out as larvae delinquents.

The spitting cobras at home

Thor's hammer, screwdriver, and crescent wrench

"I had them all removed last week and, boy, do I feel great."

Early piñatas

"Hey, everyone! Simmons here just uttered a discouraging word!"

"Letter from Lonso. ...And he sounds pretty lonely."

"Man, Ben, I'm gettin' tired of this. ...How many days now we've been eatin' this trail dust?"

Although skilled with their pillow arsenal, the Wimpodites were favorite targets of Viking attacks.

Stephen King's childhood ant farm

"Egad! It's Professor DeArmond — the epitome of evil amongst butterfly collectors!"

Trick clubbing exhibitions

"Well, look who's excited to see you back from being declawed."

"Aaaaaaaaaaaaa! Earl! ...
We've got a poultrygeist!"

"Mom! ... Earl's grossing me out with a mouthful of worms!"

At the hospital for mothers whose children stepped on sidewalk cracks

At the Old Cartoonists' Home

Warner Books now offers an exciting range of quality titles by both established and new authors which can be ordered from the following address:

Little, Brown and Company (UK) Limited,
P.O. Box 11,
Falmouth,
Cornwall TR10 9EN.

Alternatively you may fax your order to the above address. Fax No. 0326 376423.

Payments can be made as follows: cheque, postal order (payable to Little, Brown and Company) or by credit cards, Visa/Access. Do not send cash or currency. UK customers and B.F.P.O.: please allow £1.00 for postage and packing for the first book, plus 50p for the second book, plus 30p for each additional book up to a maximum charge of £3.00 (7 books plus).

Overseas customers including Ireland, please allow £2.00 for postage and packing for the first book, plus £1.00 for the second book, plus 50p for each additional book.

NAME (Block Letters) ....

ADDRESS ....

....

☐ I enclose my remittance for _____

☐ I wish to pay by Access/Visa Card

Number ☐☐☐☐☐☐☐☐☐☐☐☐☐☐☐☐

Card Expiry Date ☐☐☐☐